THE ALPHABET SONG

Retold by
STEVEN ANDERSON

Illustrated by
TAKAKO FISHER

CANTATA
LEARNING
MANKATO, MINNESOTA

WWW.CANTATALEARNING.COM

CANTATA LEARNING

MANKATO, MINNESOTA

Published by Cantata Learning
1710 Roe Crest Drive
North Mankato, MN 56003
www.cantatalearning.com

Library of Congress Control Number: 2014957028
978-1-63290-283-2 (hardcover/CD)
978-1-63290-435-5 (paperback/CD)
978-1-63290-477-5 (paperback)

The Alphabet Song by Steven Anderson
Illustrated by Takako Fisher

Book design, Tim Palin Creative
Editorial direction, Flat Sole Studio
Executive musical production and direction, Elizabeth Draper
Music arranged and produced by Steven C Music

Printed in the United States of America.

VISIT

WWW.CANTATALEARNING.COM/ACCESS-OUR-MUSIC

TO SING ALONG TO THE SONG

4

Use your finger to trace the letters as you sing along.

Then find the object that starts with each letter!

Now turn the page, and sing along.

A B C D E F G

H I J K L M N O P

10

Q R S T U V

W X Y and Z!

That was so much fun.

Let's sing it again!

a b c d e f g

15

16

h i j k l m n o p

q

r s

q r s t u v

20

W   X   Y   and Z!

Now I know my ABCs.

Next time won't you sing with me?

SONG LYRICS
The Alphabet Song

A B C D E F G

H I J K L M N O P

Q R S T U V

W X Y and Z!

That was so much fun.

Let's sing it again!

a b c d e f g

h i j k l m n o p

q r s t u v

w x y and z!

Now I know my ABCs.

Next time won't you sing with me?

The Alphabet Song

Americana
Steven C Music

GUIDED READING ACTIVITY

1. After you read this story, try saying the alphabet on your own or with a friend. Did you remember all of the letters?

2. Choose 5 letters. Draw or write about a noun (a person, place, or thing) that starts with that letter. Try to come up with nouns that are not already in this book.

3. Now try saying the alphabet backwards beginning with Z.

TO LEARN MORE

Franceschelli, Christopher. *Alphablock*. New York: Abrams, 2013.

Nunn, Daniel. *ABCs at Home*. Mankato, MN: Capstone Press, 2013.

Priddy, Roger. *Simple First Words: Let's Say Our Alphabet*. London, UK: Priddy Books, 2009.

Rissman, Rebecca. *ABCs at the Park*. Mankato, MN: Capstone Press, 2013.